MA

UNCLE MAX

SIMBA

RAFIKI

THE HYENAS

SCHOLASTIC INC.

New York   Toronto   London   Auckland   Sydney
Mexico City   New Delhi   Hong Kong   Buenos Aires

Welcome to a story of a great hero who saved the animals of the savannah—with a little help from his friends. No, it's not the story of the Lion King. It's the story of . . . me, Timon.

Let's go back to the beginning when I lived with my family in the meerkat colony. I tried digging tunnels like the rest of the family, but I never quite fit in. Take the time I added a skylight to a tunnel.

No one else liked my idea—especially my Uncle Max. I don't know why he was so angry with me. It was the first tunnel collapse I caused . . . that day.

My mother wanted me to find a place where I
fit in, so I tried being a sentry. It was my job to look
out for any dangerous hyenas. But I made one teensy
mistake. Who hasn't broken into song on sentry
duty before? I didn't exactly notice my audience.

The hyenas surprised me and caused my whole family to flee in panic.

No one was hurt, but
my career as a sentry
was over. I had to find
my place, and it wasn't
with the colony. So
I made the tough
decision to leave
home . . . to walk
out into the great
wide world.

Of course, everyone tried to
stop me. They begged me to
stay (well, maybe just
my mother), but it
was too late.

And so, I boldly went where no meerkat had gone before. I never looked back . . . because I was crying too much!

I kept going until I came to a fork in the path. "Which way should I go?" I shouted.

"That depends on what you seek," a blue-faced baboon answered. That's how I met Rafiki. He said I was looking for *hakuna matata,* a place of no worries. "To find it," he explained, "you must look beyond what you see."

"What does *that* mean?" you ask. Let me explain. It simply means . . . er . . . you must look beyond what you see.

Well, I could see a
big, pointy
rock, so I headed for that. I was
trudging through some tall grass
when I heard a strange noise.
Suddenly I found myself face to
face with a huge snout!

I was . . . surprised . . . but I quickly realized
that this big fellow, Pumbaa the warthog, was no
threat at all. In fact, he was scared of me, but I
managed to calm him down.

It turned out that Pumbaa and I were looking for the same thing—a place to call home! We made a good team. I had the brains . . . Pumbaa had, well, his own secret weapon that I would soon discover.

We both set off for the big, pointy rock,
which was called Pride Rock. We got there
just as other animals were gathering to
witness the presentation of
Simba, the future Lion
King. Of course, we didn't
know who Simba was at the time.

That's when I discovered Pumbaa's secret
weapon. I made the mistake of pulling on his tail
and . . . well, what a blast! Everyone had to bow
to the ground because the smell was so strong.
I realized that we needed to keep moving.

We looked all around for *hakuna matata*. We tried a few places including an elephant graveyard. Pumbaa was a little scared, but it didn't bother me.

After all, who would ever come to an elephant graveyard? Then we found out that hyenas would. So we decided to keep looking.

Later we found ourselves in the middle of a dry
riverbed when we heard a deep rumble. A herd of
rampaging wildebeests was headed straight for us!
"Shall we run for our lives?" Pumbaa asked me.
"Oh, yes, let's," I answered. "AHHHHHH!!!"

We thought we were safe
when we landed in a river . . .
until we went over a waterfall!

I got us safely to the riverbank. But did it bring us any closer to our goal? Well, actually it did. Instead of complaining and giving up, I stood up and looked around. Thanks to me, we had found the place of no worries, our new paradise home. It was just like the monkey had said it would be. Hot tuna frittata! Er, no . . . sorry . . . a spoon of ricotta! Arrr—wait . . . *hakuna matata!*

Once you hear that phrase, you'll never forget it.

Our lives were carefree. We ate, slept, played, slept, and ate. But then it happened! One day while bowling for buzzards, we stumbled upon a little lion cub—Simba. Of course, I wasn't scared of a lion. Nope, not me. You see, rescuing Simba wasn't the scary part—parenting was!

We had to wake up in the middle of the night . . .
feed him . . . clean him . . . catch him when he fell . . .

GEE! Nothing but a hassle! Still . . . we loved him!

As Simba grew, I taught him everything
I knew—about eating. Soon he was
ready to challenge me, his teacher,
to a fierce snail-eating contest!

I have to admit he did well. He tried his best, gave it all he had. It didn't matter who won. Okay, okay, the kid beat me.

Simba grew to be a big lion—and an even better friend. It was *hakuna matata* for the three of us. We could have gone on like that forever, but we didn't count on one thing—true love!

As soon as Nala the lioness appeared, I knew she was trouble. It would be the end of *hakuna matata*. I knew if I ruined the romance for Simba, he would thank me later. I tried every trick in the book to break them up, but nothing worked. The kid had to learn the hard way that a happy romance is awful. So I let the lovebirds sing.

And before long Nala and Simba got into a fight. Great! But then Simba left. When I asked Nala why, she told me a long, boring story about Simba being the son of the king, blah, blah, blah. In short: Simba had gone back to Pride Rock to fight some silly battle with his evil uncle Scar and the hyenas.

Nala went to help Simba, and Pumbaa followed. I decided to stay behind. Then Rafiki turned up, and we had a long talk.

Okay, okay, okay! I talked and Rafiki just
looked wise. Anyhow, I knew my friends were
going to need my wits, my courage, my leadership.
"Pumbaaaaaa!!! Wait for meee!" I shouted.

Pumbaa was so happy to see me that he almost cried like a baby. Aww, that silly little warthog.

We reached Pride Rock just in time.
The place was crawling with hyenas,
and we had to distract them so that
Simba could face Scar. Luckily, I
came up with a brilliant plan.

With a song and a hula skirt, I lured the three
meanest hyenas into a cave, and—BOOM!—off went
Pumbaa's secret weapon. The smell would teach
them not to mess with meerkats and warthogs—well,
warthogs mostly, I guess.

Suddenly two meerkats popped out of the ground. It was Ma and Uncle Max! They had been looking for me for ages. But enough of the happy reunion scene—the battle wasn't over.

High up on Pride Rock, we could see that Simba was fighting Scar. And Scar still had the hyenas helping him. Simba needed our help, and I had a plan. We needed— dare I say it?—tunnels! And Uncle Max was the best tunnel digger on earth—or below earth, actually.

The plan was as simple as it was brilliant. If Pumbaa and I could just trick those three nasty hyenas into chasing us, we could set up the best meerkat-tunnel-trap ever! Uncle Max knew how to build a tunnel, and I knew how to make it collapse!

It wasn't hard to get the hyenas' attention.
"Hey, Pumbaa," I called. "What do you call a
hyena with half a brain?"

"Beats me, Timon," Pumbaa answered. "What?"

"Gifted," I shouted. And the chase was on!

The plan went smoothly, sort of. It took a little longer than I had thought for the tunnel to be ready, so I had to keep the hyenas busy. It wasn't hard.

Finally, the tunnel was ready.
So we led the hyenas straight into
the trap, but the tunnel didn't
collapse! One of Uncle Max's
braces had stuck. Someone had to
do something. If you want something
to come crashing down, you have to do it yourself!

It worked. It actually worked! Not that I was surprised—shocked is more like it. We sent those hyenas tumbling to the bottom of Pride Rock where they belonged. Simba sent Scar crashing down there, too. Then Simba claimed his rightful place as Lion King.

My mother was proud of me and so was Uncle
Max. But what was going to happen now? They
wanted me to return to the colony. A hero's
welcome awaited me there. But what about my
new friends? This called for the greatest plan yet.

It was about time that this colony of meerkats learned something about real life—about sleeping late, having plenty to eat, and not rushing anything. I knew a place of easy living, with room for everyone!

But I had learned something, too. Home is not just a place. Home is wherever your family and friends are . . . but it doesn't hurt if it's in paradise! *Hakuna matata!*